Jerry Souva

THE BEATTY FAMILY

ANTONIO GARCIA

Here's to you aunt Cathy & your AWESOME IMAGINATION!

Connie McCleese

Julian

Peter Connie Douglas

Tom McCleese

Micah Buchin

Pat Bally

Kristen Balland (Enjoy your journey)

W.C.F.

Best of Luck with your Book Ginny

Nicole Harbin

Marsha Gilmer

Artur

ZAK

CANADIAN MACHINERY MOVERS

Berniece Louise Pegues Mullen Jackie

Dale & Vicky

Emily Good Luck Kathy

Elaine Miller

Darlene & David Buley

Ron

Diane Allen

Galley

DAVE E.

George & Shirley Yenkal

Krip Hensley

Kenny Douglas

Stefanie & Wyatt Doylas

Harmony

Elizabeth Ramos ♡

Rhonda Perry

Happiness Dad

Valerie Weather

Shawn & Tammy Kimes

Stacie

Christin & Jim Serra "JAX"

Amy

Martha Gonzalez

Kimberly Rutherford

Jim

SHEF + TIM GABE + PAYTON

Pauline Tam

Brian CARROLL

& Linzie Hunt

Josh

McIntEE

Ana Ramos

Yamileth

& Helana McKown

Sandy

Jacobs

DAVE WHITE

Dale & Debbie Justice

ARAMUS

Elizabeth Salliotte

Beth, Dan
Darren, Ryan Cox
Don & Patty Gendron
Michelle Vick
Alix M
Best wishes!!!
Natalie Tarr
Joe
Fern
Cindy Carroll Gilmer
Rebecca Tapia
Ally
Jacob
Wishing you great success!
Terry Howard
David
Jenna
Gabriella
Scott
Zoe Pearce
Maher
John Parker
Catherine Col
Josh
Gramm Nette
Sandi Schneider
Butch Young
Lexi
Love ya, Jackie Toth
Grace
SUE Sallietta
Blessing of Love, Caleb
Lizbeth Astorga
David A. Bacon
Good Luck Great Work
Jackson & Eric Cayce
Virginia Baggett
Natalie Baggett
Gina Baggett
Korey Thomas
LEXIMANOLIS
With all our love, Rodney & Jamie Lindley XO
Brandon
Michael Fuoco
JIM THOMAS
BEST WISHES
nap 10

Hope for a dream... Believe it to be...

To the patrons of my September 2009 yard sale,

Thanks for new
hope
to dream again !

Dedicated to you,

"Lukas"

"The stories that I write and illustrate are intended for children of ages three to six.

I believe this is the time in a child's life when imagination develops.

A time of why? How? When and where?

A perfect opportunity for parents to welcome their child's individual imagination.

A perfect time for stories..."

© By Cathy A. Carroll

© 2010 My Imagination Publishing LLC

Copyright 2010 My Imagination Publishing LLC. All rights reserved.

Printed and bound in the United States of America at BookMasters, Inc.

Manufactured by BookMasters
Ashland, OH (USA)
M7082   May 2010

First Edition

Library of Congress Control Number: 2010901168

For information, please contact:

My Imagination Publishing LLC
P.O. Box 1556
Southgate, MI 48195

www.myimaginationpublishing.com

ISBN-13: 9780984444304

My name is Lukas.
I am six.
I like to play alot!
With trucks and trains
and cars and planes.
But that's not all!
I got!

I have imagination
too, so I
can make pretend!
Like with this broom
here in my room
a Kingdom I'll
defend!

I knight thee Ted
my castle guard.
Let no one
through these gates!
It must be so,
for this I know,
thy enemy awaits!

Release your power
to my sword
and strength
onto my shield !
Then lead with me
to victory
upon the battlefield !

Behold your king
with shield and sword
upon thy trusted steed!
We two as one
in fear of none
shall fight with might
and speed!

Lukas!

Oh o !

Let's finish cleaning
up your room
and put your toys away.
Then in the tub
to rub a dub dub !
It's bed time soon
ok ? .

I cleaned my room
and found this toy.
I put away the rest.
Together we
will search the sea
and find a
treasure chest!

I am the captain
of this ship!
I sail across the sea!
In search of gold
to have and hold.
Where could this
treasure be?

The weather started
getting rough !
The waves are ten feet tall !
They're crashing in
and I begin
to slip and then
I fall !

Down and down
and down I go !
I tumble through the sea !
Until I rest
on a treasure chest
here waiting
just for me !

When I opened
up the chest
I saw the mother lode!
A hundred trillion
billion million
gazillion
chunks of gold!

Lukas !

oh o !

Don't forget to
brush your teeth.
And comb your hair Ok?
It's getting near
your bed time dear.
There's little time
to play !

Soon I have to
go to bed.
But, just before I do!
I've got to sing
and do my thing
and rock the socks
off you!

Lukas !

oh o !

Here's your P.J.'s.
Put them on.
Then hop into your bed.
It's time again
to tuck you in.
Let's go now
sleepy head !

Close your eyes
and go to sleep.
Please hush now. Not a peep !
Sweet dreams. Night night.
Now you sleep tight !
Don't let the
bed bugs bite !

Bed bugs?

Imagination!

The End ?

The
End ?

There is no End to Imagination!

see ya!

Lord
Bless this
Cheryl Summers

BEST OF LUCK
Lino Small

Good
Luck!
Angie Carroll

Best Wishes to my
Good Friends on my First Book!
Best of Luck Family
The Trainor Family
Dave, Sandi & Alyssa Jill

Patricia Buck

K.
M. Christine Bowen
"09"

Ray Small

Hardwork Jim
Ben Burke Nerd

Butch & Marlon Felipe
(Philippines)

Ray Well

Working Well

Elena Ramos

Andrew & Laura
Decker

Doug Carl

Kathy Wieland
Hoppenworth

God Luck Linda
Diane & Don
Luke

Ken Ellis

Jim Haggard

Good luck
Ve Reece
Garry Reece

Kathy! complete
confidence in this
Book

Good luck with Jamieson
many more from Jamieson
Kaven

M. Crosby

From your lips
to God's Ears.
Wm Bruun

At
Good
Work.
Elizabeth
Matt H

Sue Kyntz

Best Wishes,
Mary Lou
Russell

Sue Monter

Amber
Young

Joseph M. Raymond

John Dupre

Fast Eddie

Hummi
Lauri M

CHARLES Buc

Cathy! Good Luck with
your books!!
Love ya
Frank Young
Cindy I Love you

OJoculY
Maker14

Marino & Ruth & Lexi.
Manolis
Allen Park

Good Luck... But more
than luck... God Bless

GENE
FRONK
God Bless,
Joe & Kay
Pagel
XO

Don & Glenda Barganus
Young
Dan

Roman Stanowski

Jennifer Stanowski

Erik Szlachetka & kids

Arianna Michele Cook

Cathy— We are so proud!! Love it
Donna, Dave, Christina & Caroline Grachek 42009?

God Bless You Hammett

Mcmellow 2009

Sandy Dubycki Enjoy your drive-thru lady! 2009!

Robbie Orme

Charlie & Barb Abbott

Bob

Melissa Green

Tom Green JR

Best of luck Robert Douglas + Brad

Maria

Good Luck Loyd

Theresa Sciarotti

Luck to you Neal

Tom Haggard

Godfrey M McCumber

Mayra D. Espinoza
Jose L Espinoza

Walter Liz Pinsley

John Hergott

Samuel Koehe

JoAnn Douglas

Jennie Skinner Good luck! Kim Tressa

Jenn Ames

Lodi McCumber

Scottie, Marla & Sheldon!

With love and Hope, but even more Faith, Christina Grachek

Denise Ramos

Angel Ramos

Bill Douglas

Suzanne DuVall

Cayden Azviela Jordan

John Craanen

Bon Jarols

Annette Hunter (G-Ba!)

MORE BLESSINGS

Maria Apati

The Hall Family

Kevin Hoksombach

Sue Shedden

Nichola Davis

Gayle Cox
Good Luck! Stan~ Lucy Klos

God Bless! Judy Aiken

Maria Deane

Good Luck! Suzie Hazdovicz

You're great Wilma

Bill Staggs
RB IV

Rosa Garcia